This annual belongs to

Day out with Thomas™

Day Out With Thomas
Thomas the Tank Engine & Friends
Based on the Railway Series
by Reverend W Awdry
© 2006 Gullane (Thomas) Limited
A HIT Entertainment Company

Days out with Thomas invite children, parents and grandparents to enter the magical world of Thomas & Friends at heritage railways throughout the UK.

Family visitors to our activity-filled events can meet, touch and ride behind their favourite Number 1 blue engine. Sir Topham Hatt, The Fat Controller, is also in attendance at all events to ensure that the engines are well-behaved and that Thomas is being Really Useful.

Meet your favourite classic character, Thomas the Tank Engine, at a heritage railway near you. Information and ticket details can be found on our website www.thomasandfriends.com.

THOMAS & FRIENDS™

Contents

Thomas the Tank Engine & Friends

A BRITT ALLCROFT COMPANY PRODUCTION

Based on The Railway Series by The Rev W Awdry

© Gullane (Thomas) LLC 2006

Photographs © Gullane (Thomas) Limited 2006

EGMONT

We bring stories to life

First published in Great Britain 2006 by Egmont UK Limited
239 Kensington High Street, London W8 6SA

ISBN 978 1 4052 2608 0
ISBN 1 4052 2608 0
1 0 9 8 7 6 5 4 3
Printed in Italy
All rights reserved

Stories based on original scripts by Abi Grant, Paul Larson, James Mason and Marc Seal.

"Hello! I'm Sir Topham Hatt, but everyone calls me **The Fat Controller.** I'm in charge of the railway on the Island of Sodor. It's my job to make sure the engines arrive on time and take passengers where they want to go. Some very special engines help me. Come and meet them!"

The Sodor railway engines

"**Thomas** is my Really Useful Number 1 engine. He's a hard-working little tank engine and he works on his own branch line with his coaches, Annie and Clarabel. They take workmen to and from the Quarry."

"**Edward** is the blue Number 2 engine. He's a bit older than the others but he's very reliable. You can read his story on page 60."

"**Henry** is very long, very fast – and very strong! He's my smart green Number 3 engine."

"**Gordon** is the big blue Number 4 Express. He's the fastest and most powerful of all my engines."

"**James** is the Really splendid Number 5 engine. You can read about the day when he got new trucks on page 14."

"**Percy**, Number 6, is a hard-working little engine who loves puffing around the Yard with the trucks. He knows just how to handle them, even the troublesome ones!"

"**Toby** is the Number 7 tram engine. He's a bit old-fashioned but he and his coach, Henrietta, still do very useful work on the Quarry line."

"**Emily** is Really Useful because she can do all sorts of jobs. She has dark green paint and shiny brass fittings."

"**Salty** works at Brendam Docks where he shunts the trains in place behind the engines."

"**Cranky** is a crane who works at the Docks with Salty. His job is to load and unload things from the ships and trains."

"**Bill** and **Ben** are bright yellow twin engines. They work on the line between the clay pits and the Harbour."

"**Harvey** is the dark red Number 27 crane engine. He's Really Useful when engines run off the tracks, as you'll see in the story on page 14."

The Narrow Gauge railway engines

"Hello! My name is Mr Percival, but most people call me **The Thin Controller**. I look after the Narrow Gauge railway for The Fat Controller. I'll tell you all about my engines. I'm very proud of them!"

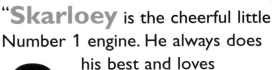 "**Skarloey** is the cheerful little Number 1 engine. He always does his best and loves working with his best friend, Rheneas, on the steep Mountain Railway."

"**Rheneas** is the Number 2 engine. He's quite old and sometimes breaks down, but we always get him mended because he's so Useful. You can read his story on page 46."

"**Peter Sam** is Number 4. He's green and though the others tease him sometimes, they love him really. He's always ready to do late hours or extra work."

"**Rusty** is the bright orange diesel engine, Number 5. He loves hard work and adventures and you can read all about his special whistle on page 22."

"**Duncan** is Number 6. He's a gold engine who has a mind of his own! He can be a bit rude at times and doesn't always like being told what to do!"

Thomas' new trucks

It was another busy day on the Island of Sodor. Thomas was in the Yard, shunting his trucks. It was hard work and he was **_huffing_** and **_puffing_**, **_biffing_** and **_bashing_** the trucks. They were old and rusty and Thomas was tired out.

When James puffed into the Yard, he was looking very pleased with himself. "Look!" he huffed proudly. "The Fat Controller has given me shiny new trucks. They're **MUCH** nicer than your old ones, Thomas!"

Thomas looked at the trucks. James was right, the new ones were much nicer than his. "It's not fair!" said Thomas sadly. "I want shiny new trucks, too!"

The next morning when Thomas puffed out of Tidmouth Sheds, The Fat Controller had a surprise for him. "Your trucks are too old for the heavy loads you pull, Thomas," he said. "You're going to have some new ones, just like James."

Thomas was very pleased when he collected his trucks. He puffed off with his new trucks proudly behind.

As he steamed into Brendam Docks, James was showing off his new trucks to Bill and Ben.

"**Peep!**" said Thomas, blowing his whistle. "I've got new trucks, too!"

"Yours are even shinier than James'!" puffed Ben.

That made James cross. "Your trucks are shiny now, Thomas," he huffed. "But you won't be able to keep them as clean and shiny as mine!"

"Oh yes I will!" said Thomas. "You wait and see. I'll have the cleanest, shiniest trucks on the whole Island!"

Next day, Thomas took his new trucks to the Quarry.

"**Must-keep-my-trucks-clean! Must-keep-my-trucks-clean!**" he puffed.

James was there collecting slate. "Look, I haven't got a speck of dust on me **OR** my trucks!" he boasted.

"I can do that, too!" said Thomas. He backed under a hopper but his naughty new trucks rolled back a bit too far and – **whooosh!** – slate poured down all over the tracks, and all over Thomas!

The new trucks laughed, and so did James. "Your trucks don't look so shiny now!" he huffed.

Next, Thomas took his new trucks to the Coaling Plant. This time he backed under the coal hopper VERY slowly. But the naughty trucks rolled too far again and the coal landed all over the tracks. Thomas was covered in coal dust and his new trucks were dirtier than ever!

The next morning, Thomas puffed into Wellsworth Yard. He saw his new trucks **AND** his old ones and had an idea. "I'll use my old trucks for the messy coal, and keep my new ones clean," he decided.

He took his old trucks to the Docks, but on the way there was trouble! A coupling broke – **SNAP!** – and the trucks rattled along behind him all by themselves!

"**Cinders and ashes!**" cried Thomas. He put on his brakes but he stopped so quickly that the trucks bumped into him and all the coal spilled out on to the tracks. Thomas was stuck. He couldn't move!

When The Fat Controller arrived with Harvey, he was not pleased! "These trucks are too old for pulling coal," he said. "You've caused a delay, Thomas!"

Harvey moved the spilled coal and Thomas raced off to collect his **NEW** trucks.

When he got back, the crew filled them with coal.

Soon the new trucks were very dirty. But as Thomas raced to the Docks they were no trouble at all.

They rolled easily up the hills ... They rattled quickly down the hills ... And they sang all the way to the Docks! They were happy!

Thomas understood. "My new trucks **LIKE** being messy," he said. "They have more fun when they're dirty! My trucks would rather be **USEFUL** than **CLEAN!**"

When James got to the Docks and his trucks saw how happy Thomas' were, they decided they wanted some fun too.

James backed up to Cranky to load melons for the market but his trucks stopped **VERY** quickly.

"Hold back! Hold back!" they laughed as the melons landed on James. *Squelch! Squish! Squash!* What a sticky mess!

"Bother!" huffed James but his trucks just laughed, and so did Thomas.

"Peep!" said Thomas. "Your trucks would rather be **USEFUL** than clean, just like mine!"

Count with Thomas

Little Thomas had to pull a lot of heavy trucks!

Count the number of trucks in the big picture, then colour in the same number of trucks below. Write the number in the box.

What a lot of balloons!

Use blue, yellow, red and green pens to colour in a balloon for each one you can see in the picture. Count each set of balloons and write the number in each box.

2   8   3   3

ANSWER: There are 2 blue, 3 yellow, 8 red and 3 green balloons.

Tuneful toots

The little engines who work on the Narrow Gauge mountain railway are always busy! They go **up** the hills and **down** the hills, all day long!

Rusty likes puffing along by the lake best. He likes to toot his horn there because the sound echoes around the hills.

Rusty's horn is special because it has two notes, a high one and a low one: **"Toot! Toot!"**

Rusty liked his toot, but the other engines didn't. They thought it was the most awful noise they had ever heard!

One morning Mr Percival, The Thin Controller of the Narrow Gauge railway, had news for the engines. "Sir Topham and Lady Hatt are visiting our railway tonight," he told them. "And a brass band is coming to play for them!"

The engines were very excited. Rusty loved brass-band music and couldn't wait to hear it.

There was a lot to do before the visit, though!

Skarloey and Rheneas brought tables and chairs and Duncan and Peter Sam helped too.

Rusty thought he had the best job of all! He was going to take the members of the brass band on a trip before the concert started. When he pulled into the Transfer Yards to collect them, he tooted his horn happily: *"Toot! Toot!"*

Thomas heard the toot when he arrived with the bandstand. "What was that lovely sound?" he asked.

"It was Rusty," Peter Sam told him. "He thinks his horn is special, but we don't like it!"

"**Wheesh!**" said Thomas. "Well **I** do!"

When the brass band players were on board, Rusty pulled out of the station. "Don't be back late!" called The Thin Controller, but Rusty didn't hear him. He was too busy tooting his horn: *"Toot! Toot! Toot! Toot! Toot! Toot!"*

Rusty took the brass band to the viaduct and the bridge. He was so happy that he forgot all about the concert and set off for the lake! **Clickety-clack!** went Rusty as he huffed past the old castle: *"Toot! Toot!"*

But suddenly – **clang!** – Rusty stopped. He had run out of fuel!

"How will we get back?" said the leader of the band. "How will Mr Percival know where we are?"

Rusty tooted. "If you all play loudly and I toot my horn extra hard, the sound will echo all the way back to the Yards," he said. "Then The Thin Controller will know where we are."

The leader of the band waved his baton and the band began to play. Then Rusty tooted his horn as loudly as he could:

"Toot! Toot!"
"Toot! Toot!"
"Toot! Toot!"

Thomas and The Fat Controller and Lady Hatt were waiting in the Transfer Yards when they heard the sounds.

"That's Rusty and the brass band!" puffed Thomas. "They must be in trouble. If we follow the sounds we'll find them."

The brass band kept playing and Rusty kept tooting until he saw engine lamps coming towards them along the track.

Soon all the engines were at the lake, and so was The Fat Controller. "We will have the brass band concert here!" he said.

"We heard your horn, Rusty!" said Peter Sam.

"That's how we found you!" said Duncan.

"Because you have a really special tooty horn!" said Skarloey.

Rusty was very pleased and when all the engines blew their whistles – **"PEEP!"** – Rusty tooted louder than ever before:

"Toot! Toot!"

Rusty's picture jigsaw

Rusty was very pleased that his job was to take the members of the brass band for a ride. But he forgot to bring them back in time!

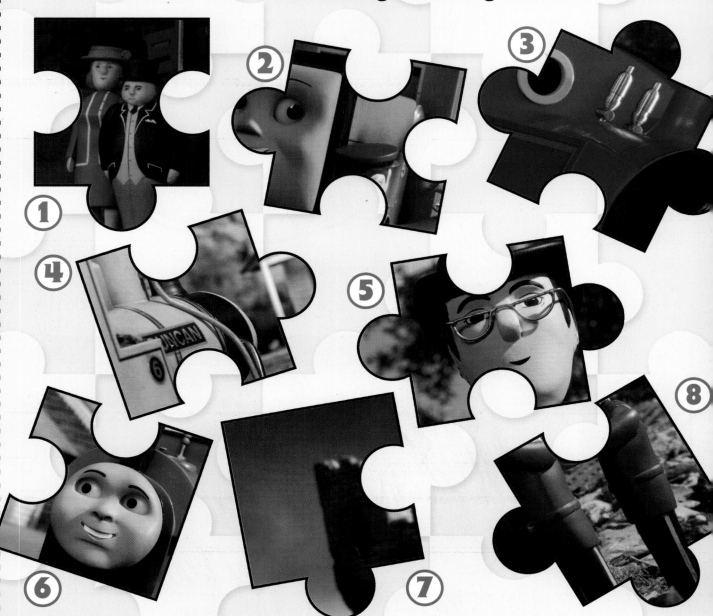

The little jigsaw puzzle pieces are all mixed up!
Which pieces will complete the big picture on the next page?
You can draw and colour them in if you like.

Saving Edward

It was summer on Sodor and the engines were busy taking passengers and goods all over the Island. Thomas, Gordon and the other engines were happy to be so Useful.

But Edward wasn't happy. He was worried because he didn't feel well. He wheezed as he puffed along and steam hissed out of his cylinders.

One morning, The Fat Controller went to Tidmouth Sheds. He had jobs for Edward and Thomas. "Edward, I want you to take a special delivery of fruit and vegetables from the Docks to Knapford," he said. "Thomas, I want you to go to the Docks and shunt Edward's trucks."

Thomas and Edward puffed to the water tower to take on water. But Edward just couldn't stop wheezing.

"You don't sound well," said Thomas.

"I can't get up steam properly," hissed Edward. "But please don't tell anyone, Thomas. I don't want The Fat Controller to know."

Edward puffed to the Docks but it took him a long time to get there because he could only go slowly. As he wheezed along he felt more and more worried. What if he was too weak to pull his train? He would be no use at all.

"Must-keep-going! Must-keep-going!" he wheezed.

At the Docks, Thomas shunted Edward's trucks for him and soon he was ready to go.

Edward puffed as hard as he could but the train moved very slowly – then it stopped. "I'm sorry," he wheezed. "I'm not a Really Useful engine any more. I'll just have to go for scrap."

Thomas wanted to help his old friend. "I'll do my other jobs first," he told him. "Then I'll come back and pull the train for you."

Poor Edward! He could only stand and wait for Thomas to come back ...

Thomas did his other jobs as fast as he could. **"Hurry-up! Hurry-up!"** he told the Troublesome Trucks. **"What-for? What-for?"** snapped the trucks.

"For Edward!" said Thomas, **biffing** them into a siding.

When Thomas got back to the Docks, Edward was very pleased to see him.

"I'll be back for you soon," said Thomas, then puffed off with Edward's train.

But Edward's train was very heavy and Thomas had been working hard all day. He was very tired but he didn't want to let Edward down, so he **puffed** and **chuffed** and **huffed** along, as fast as he could.

When Thomas pulled into
Knapford Station, The Fat
Controller was waiting. "Why
are you pulling this train?" he
asked. "Where is Edward?"

"Er, he took on the wrong
sort of coal ..." said Thomas.

"THE
WRONG
SORT OF
COAL!"

boomed The Fat
Controller.
"Nonsense,
Thomas! I'll
speak to
Edward
about this
later!"

He was so cross that
he gave poor Thomas
another job to do.

When Thomas didn't come
back for him, Edward wheezed
slowly home.

He stopped for a rest and Gordon told him what The Fat Controller had said to Thomas.

Edward felt very bad. He wanted to put things right, so he **hissed** and **wheezed** all the way to Knapford. His fire felt feeble. His wheels felt weak, but he didn't give up.

When he puffed into the station he spoke to The Fat Controller. "It's all my fault," he said. "I asked Thomas not to tell anyone I couldn't work. I was afraid of being no use and being sent for scrap."

"You should always tell me if you have a problem," said The Fat Controller. "You are a hard-working engine, Edward. A Really Useful engine. You must go to the Fitter's Yard right away. They'll mend you and you'll be back at work in no time at all."

Thomas went with Edward, who was happy again now that he knew he'd soon be as good as new.

Thomas and Edward had both learned an important lesson that day.

"Even when it's hard ..." said Edward.

"It's always best to tell the truth!" said Thomas. **"Peeeep!"**

Spot the difference

Thomas was pleased when The Fat Controller gave him an important job. But poorly Edward wasn't pleased at all. He was afraid he would be sent for scrap!

These two pictures look the same but there are 5
things that are different in picture 2.
Look very carefully – can you spot them all?

Thomas' milkshake muddle

Once a year, the children who live on the Island of Sodor are invited to a special summer party! At this year's party there was going to be ice cream and cakes.

At Tidmouth Sheds The Fat Controller was choosing who should take the children to the party. It was a special job that all the engines wanted to do.

Thomas hoped it would be him – but The Fat Controller chose Emily!

"There is another job for one of you," The Fat Controller added. "But it is a job that has to be done very carefully, so I need a very reliable engine."

"Me, Sir!" peeped Thomas. "I'll do it!"

"Very well," said The Fat Controller.

Soon, Thomas was on his way to the Dairy. He was going there to collect milk to take to the Ice-cream Factory where it would be made into ice cream for the party.

Thomas was coupled to trucks full of large milk churns. "Take the churns to the Ice-cream Factory," the Dairy Manager told him. "But you must go VERY slowly."

"I will," said Thomas, and he set off chuffing slowly and steadily.

When Thomas stopped at a signal Emily pulled up next to him. "Hello, slowcoach!" she whistled.

"I'm not slow!" said Thomas. "I'm being **STEADY** and **RELIABLE!**"

Emily sniffed. "If you weren't such a slowcoach The Fat Controller would have given you **MY** job!" she said. "I'm fast **AND** reliable. That's why **I'M** taking the children to the party!"

Thomas was cross. "I can be as fast as you!" he huffed.

"Prove it!" said Emily. "I'll race you to the next signal."

The signal turned green and Emily steamed away. Thomas raced after her as fast as his pistons would pump!

As he raced along, the milk churns **rattled** and **rocked** and **clinked** and **clanked**. They **biffed** and **bashed** and **clacked** and **chinked**.

At the next signal, Thomas was way ahead of Emily! He was so pleased that he raced off to the Ice-cream Factory. He forgot all about going slowly and steadily!

Thomas got to the factory in record time. The Manager was very pleased – until he looked inside one of the churns. "This milk is almost butter!" he said. "Did it rattle around? If you shake milk about it turns into butter."

The Manager was angry with Thomas. "You must get more milk from the Dairy," he told him. "And this time go **SLOWLY!**"

When Thomas got to the Dairy The Fat Controller was there. "The Dairy has run out of butter for the children's cakes," he told Thomas. "You must go to the farm to collect some more."

Thomas decided to take the milk to the Ice-cream Factory first. This time he went slowly and carefully. When he got there the Manager told him to take the old milk churns back to the Dairy.

Poor Thomas! How would he get to the farm now?

Suddenly he had an idea. The baker needed butter, and what was in the milk churns was **almost** butter, so ...

Thomas steamed back even faster than before!

He huffed up Gordon's Hill and chuffed down to the valley.

He **raced** like a rocket and **wheeshed** like the wind.

The milk churns **rattled** and **rolled**. They **clanked** and **crashed** and **biffed** and **bashed** into each other.

Thomas raced to the station and blew his whistle long and hard:

"Peeeeeeeeep!"

"Look inside the churns!" Thomas told the Baker. Now the milk was **BUTTER** and there was enough to make lots and lots of cakes for the party!

The Fat Controller went to speak to Thomas when he heard what he had done.

Thomas thought he might get a telling off, but The Fat Controller was very pleased with him. "Thomas, you've saved the children's party!" he boomed. "You are the most **RELIABLE** engine on the whole Island!"

Later on the children were enjoying their party when the special Guest of Honour arrived.

Can you guess who it was?

Yes – it was **THOMAS!**

Thomas' picture puzzle

Clever Thomas made sure there was milk to make ice cream and butter to make cakes. The Fat Controller was so pleased with him that Thomas was the special Guest of Honour at the children's party.

1

a   b   c   d   e   f

The big pictures are from Thomas' story. Which of the little pictures can you see in the big ones? Write ✓ for yes or ✗ for no in each wheel.

a   b   c   d   e   f

45

Rheneas and the dinosaur

Rheneas and Skarloey are best friends who work on the Narrow Gauge Mountain Railway.

They like working together, especially when they're shunting trucks. They **biff** them and **bash** them, then they **bash** them and **biff** them, all day long.

One summer, people from the Sodor Museum found some very old bones. When they put them all together they made something very exciting – the skeleton of a **dinosaur**!

A man came to Sodor to take pictures of the dinosaur and Thomas took him to the Transfer Yards where Mr Percival, The Thin Controller, was talking to his engines.

"The dinosaur is going to the Sodor Museum," he said. "I need two very **careful** engines to take it there."

"We can be **really careful**," puffed Rheneas. "Just watch us!"

Rheneas shunted some trucks together very gently, but Skarloey was so excited that he forgot about being careful and **crashed** and **bashed** the trucks into each other!

The Thin Controller was NOT pleased. "You are not careful engines!" he said. "I will choose two others to collect the dinosaur."

Poor Rheneas! He really wanted the job! "I CAN be careful!" he said. "Please let me try. **PLEASE**!"

"Very well," said The Thin Controller.

Rheneas was happy now — but Skarloey wasn't. "I'm sorry I biffed the trucks like that," he whistled. "Can we take the dinosaur together, Rheneas?"

"**NO!**" said Rheneas. "I'll show The Thin Controller I can do it **on my own**."

Rheneas had to take coal to the Station Houses but the trucks were very heavy now that he was working on his own.

His pistons **pounded** and his axles **ached** ... but Rheneas kept going.

"**Must-take-the-dinosaur! Must-take-the-dinosaur!**" he puffed.

Later on, The Thin Controller spoke to Rheneas. "You have worked very hard today pulling the heavy trucks on your own, and you did it carefully," he said. "That's why I have decided that you can collect the dinosaur skeleton. Are you sure you can do it on your own?"

"Oh, yes, Sir!" whistled Rheneas happily and he rushed off to collect the dinosaur skeleton.

But when he saw it he got a surprise. The dinosaur was big, **very big**! **Very big indeed**.

Rheneas coupled up to the flatbed and pulled with all his puff.

He pulled the skeleton through Middle Station and everyone cheered.

But when he huffed up a steep hill, Rheneas went slowly because the flatbed was too heavy and his puff was going. His pistons could hardly pump and he became slower and slower and slower ... until he **rolled back down the hill**!

"Oh, no," said Rheneas sadly. "I'll never get the dinosaur to the Transfer Yards now. I wish Skarloey was here to help me."

Just then Skarloey came round a bend in the line. He was very surprised when he saw the skeleton blocking the way!

"Out of my way!" he tooted.

"Can you help me, Skarloey?" asked Rheneas. "The dinosaur is too heavy for me. I was silly to think I could pull it on my own. It needs two engines. From now on I want us to work together, always."

Skarloey wasn't sure at first, but when he saw how sad his friend was he buffered up to the flatbed and they pushed the dinosaur up the hill together.

Rheneas and Skarloey got the dinosaur skeleton to the Transfer Yards just as Thomas arrived with the photographer. He took a picture of them all with it.

Now Rheneas and Skarloey know what the best job of all is: working with your **best friend**!

Dinosaur dig

When people from the Sodor Museum dug up some old bones they put them all together to make something very exciting – the skeleton of a **dinosaur**!

Count the things in the picture and write a number in each box.

| 1 | 2 | 4 | 3 | 1 |

Now draw a picture of the dinosaur skeleton and write your name on the line.

The dinosaur skeleton by

Ng Jing Jing

53

Thomas and the statue

You can read this story about Thomas! The little pictures will help you. When you see the pictures of Thomas and his friends, say their names.

The Fat Controller

Thomas

Edward

Percy

Henry

Gordon

One day,  asked  to collect a railway statue from the Docks. "I wonder what it looks like?" said . "I'll tell you when I come back," said . When he collected the statue from the Docks it was covered in a cloth, but  saw a funnel shape at the front. "I think it's a statue of ME!" said . "It's my shape!"

That night  couldn't wait to tell the

other engines about the statue. But  was

fast asleep, and so was . Not even little

 was awake. Next day  talked

and talked and talked about his statue. He

boasted about it to  and the others.

 was being a real show-off!

", please stop talking about the statue!" said . "You're just showing off and being boastful!" 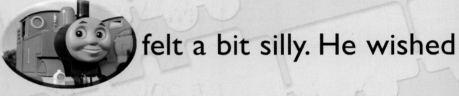 felt a bit silly. He wished he hadn't talked about himself so much! When heavy snow fell  told  that he would clear the tracks so  and the other engines could go to see

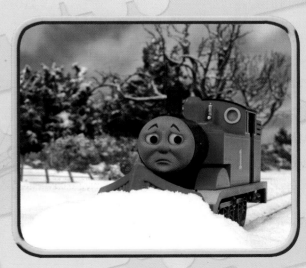

the statue being put up.

 wanted to show  and

and the others that he was sorry for showing off.

When ,  and the other engines

saw the statue they got a surprise. "It's not ,

after all!" said . "It's all of us!" peeped

. Just then  arrived. "I'm

glad the statue isn't only of me!" said .

"We're ALL important,

aren't we? PEEEP!"

Name the engines

Thomas told The Fat Controller that he would clear the snowy tracks so the other engines could go to see the statue. He wanted to say sorry for being such a show-off!

Can you point to the engines and say their names?

EDWARD   EMILY   GORDON   HENRY

JAMES   PERCY   THOMAS

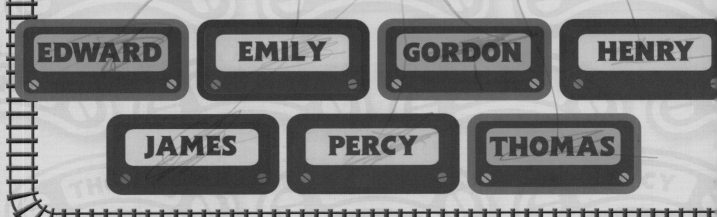

ANSWER: Left to right, the engines are: Edward, Emily, Gordon, Percy, Thomas, Henry and James.

Can you find the names of the engines in the word puzzle? They are spelled out from side to side and from top to bottom.

A	R	L	Q	P	I	J	H
Z	T	B	K	E	E	X	E
X	H	G	O	R	D	O	N
E	O	C	F	C	W	N	R
E	M	I	L	Y	A	N	Y
J	A	M	E	S	R	O	P
E	S	D	G	H	D	O	Y

Draw a line through each name you find, and tick the list.

EDWARD ☑   EMILY ☑
GORDON ☑   HENRY ☑
JAMES ☑   PERCY ☑
THOMAS ☑

Keeping up with James

It was winter on the Island of Sodor and the hills and houses, bridges and branch lines, stations and signalboxes were all covered in a white snowy blanket.

Workmen were fitting the engines with snowploughs in the Fitter's Yard. "We have to keep the railway running so you must work in pairs," The Fat Controller told the engines.

"**Gordon** will work with **Emily**, **Toby** will work with **Henry**, **Percy** will work with **Thomas** – and **James** will work with **Edward**," said The Fat Controller. "Now remember, the tracks are very icy and you must all **take care!**"

The Fat Controller had something else to tell them. "When the lines are clear I want one of you to take the Presents Train to the Winter Party at Knapford."

ALL the engines wanted to do that special job – especially James. But he didn't want to do it with Edward. "He's an old slowcoach," he huffed. "He'll just slow me down!"

Thomas felt sorry for Edward. "Don't worry," he told him. "There's more to being a Really Useful Engine than being fast."

Later, James and Edward were clearing the lines to Knapford. Edward chugged along slowly and steadily.

He wasn't fast enough for James, who huffed past him and peeped loudly.

"Hurry up!"

James rushed past Gordon and Emily.

"Slow down!" called Gordon. **"Take care!"** cried Emily.

But James took no notice. He was thinking about the Presents Train, not the icy tracks, and his wheels began to slip and slide! **"Whoooooaah!"** he cried as he went faster and faster. He liked going fast so he slid all the way to Knapford Station, where men were putting up the Christmas decorations.

Edward arrived much later. "Trust you to be late!" James huffed. "We're taking coal trucks to the mines and you are to be the back engine. I'll show you how to go fast!"

As soon as Edward buffered up to the trucks, James pulled out and raced off. **"Must-be-first! Must-be-first!"** he puffed.

When he got to the top of Gordon's Hill, his boiler **bubbled** and his pistons **pumped**. Then his wheels started to slip and slide on the icy tracks and he sped down the hill.

"Wheee!" cried James. "This is how you go fast!"

Poor Edward was pulled down the hill. He put on his brakes as hard as he could but then **his** wheels started to slip and **both** of them slid all the way down the hill!

"You must slow down and **take care**," Edward told James.

"I **am** taking care," said James. "Taking care to go **fast** and finish my jobs **first**. Then I'm going to pull the **Presents Train!**"

James set off for the Docks, dreaming of the Presents Train. **"Finish-first! Finish-first!"** he puffed, going faster and faster.

When he came to a bend in the track James put on his brakes to slow down but his wheels slipped and slid. **"Oh, my!"** he cried.

Edward braked so hard that his wheels **wobbled** and his axles **squeaked**. But it was too late, and James and two of the coal trucks came off the rails!

"Bust my buffers!" said James.

When The Fat Controller arrived on Salty he was **NOT** pleased with James and Edward. "You did not **take care** as I told you!" he boomed.

James felt bad. "The crash wasn't Edward's fault," he said. "He wanted to slow down but I wanted to go fast so I could pull the Presents Train."

"Well you won't be pulling it now!" said The Fat Controller. "Edward, **YOU** can pull the Presents Train. I'll find a back engine for you."

"If I promise to go slowly and **take care**, can I be Edward's back engine?" asked James.

"Very well," said The Fat Controller.

Edward and James collected the Presents Train from the Docks. **"Slow down!"** called Edward when they came to icy patches on the track. And this time **James slowed down**. **"Put on your brakes!"** called Edward when they ran down Gordon's Hill. And this time **James put on his brakes**.

The children were waiting at Knapford Station and when Edward and James steamed in, everyone cheered.

"Thank you for letting me help, Edward," said James happily. "You are a **Really Useful Engine!**"

The Fat Controller's quiz

"I have some questions for you. See if you can answer them. Look back through the book to find the answers. **Good luck!**"

1. This picture is from the story "Keeping up with James" on page 60.

a Who helped Edward with the Presents Train? *James*

b At which station did the children have their Christmas party? *Knapf*

c Who called Edward a "Really Useful Engine"? *James*

2. Which of the Narrow Gauge engines goes, **"Toot! Toot!"?**

Rusty

3. What is the name of the crane who loads and unloads things at the Docks?

cranky

4. What are the names of these twin engines? And who's who?

bilt
ben

5. What is The Thin Controller's real name? Is it:
a Mr Peters
b Mr Percival or
c Mr Parker?

6. In "Rheneas and the dinosaur" on page 46, which engine helped Rheneas to pull the dinosaur skeleton?

Scarloey

7. What is the name of the Number 27 crane engine? Is it:
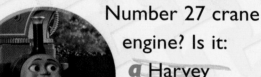
a Harvey
b Henry or
c Harry?

8. What colour is Emily's paintwork?

Dark green

9. In the story "Thomas' new trucks" on page 14, which engine got new trucks before Thomas?

James

10. Which engine got himself in a "milkshake muddle"?

Thomas

"Check your answers, then turn to the next page for a special surprise!"

ANSWERS: 1. a, James, b. Knapford, c, James; 2. Rusty; 3. Cranky; 4. Bill and Ben (Ben is in front!); 5. b, Mr Percival; 6. Skarloey; 7. a, Harvey; 8. green; 9. James; 10. Thomas.

67

"Well done!" says The Fat Controller. "You know all about Thomas and the other railway engines.

You are

Thomas' special friend

Fill in your special friend award certificate. Draw **your** picture in the space and write your name on the name plate. Now add your number in the little box."

THOMAS
1

Thomas' special friend

Jing

7

Look out for puzzles, colouring and stories in these Really Useful Magazines!

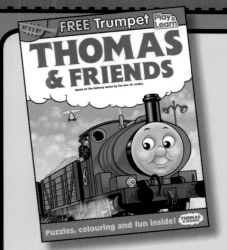

FREE Trumpet **Play & Learn**

THOMAS & FRIENDS

Based on The Railway Series by the Rev. W. Awdry.

Puzzles, colouring and fun inside!

FREE Box of Stickers

THOMAS & FRIENDS

Based on The Railway Series by The Rev. W. Awdry.

splendid stories from THOMAS inside!

FREE **Play Watches**

THOMAS & FRIENDS

Classic story collection

Based on the Railway notes by the Rev. W. Awdry.

Play & Learn
Packed with puzzles and activities. Every fortnight.

THOMAS & FRIENDS
Read the latest stories straight from Sodor Island! Every fortnight.

Thomas' Express Special
A collection of classic stories. On sale every four weeks.

Free gift with every issue!

Can you help the little engines find their way to The Fat Controller?

On sale in all good newsagents and supermarkets now!